In this first nontechnical book to appear on
the topic of feathers, Hilda Simon reveals
what science has learned about these
unique skin structures which enable birds
to fly. The book begins with the mystery of
how feathers evolved, ranging from concepts of the hypothetical reptilian ancestor
of birds to the habits of the Australian
brush turkey and the South American
hoatzin, whose peculiar behavior today
yields clues about the way of life, 130 million years ago, of the earliest known bird,
Archaeopteryx. Miss Simon tells how adult
feathers develop from tiny buds in the skin
of the embryo and what distinguishes one
type of feather from another, relating their
marvelously complex structures to distinctive functions. The most fascinating pas-
sages concern the bewildering array of
colors and patterns found among the thousands of bird species, explaining how some
colors are produced chemically and others
physically by surface structures, and what
causes dazzling iridescent colors such as
those of the hummingbird. There is also an
interesting sampling of unusual plumage
—the magnificent ornamental feathers of
exotic pheasants, birds of paradise, and the
strange lyrebird.

Throughout the book are Miss Simon's
exquisitely beautiful color illustrations to
delight the eye, together with meticulously
drawn diagrams to support the informa-
tive text.

FEATHERS

plain and fancy

FEATHERS

plain and fancy

fancy

by Hilda Simon
Illustrated by the author

THE VIKING PRESS   NEW YORK

To Beatrice Rosenfeld
in gratitude for her enthusiastic and sensitive
help and cooperation

598   1. Feathers
      2. Birds

Acknowledgments

I gratefully acknowledge my debt for information in the preparation of this book provided by the work of Adolf Portmann, professor of zoology at Basel University, Tracy I. Storer, professor of zoology at the University of California, Oliver L. Austin, Jr., of the Florida State Museum, J. Lear Grimmer, director of the National Zoological Garden in Washington, D.C., Crawford H. Greenewalt, nature photographer, the German zoologists L. Hoffmann, R. Goehringer, and A. Gerber, and the German scientific journal *Natur und Museum*. I also want to express my deep appreciation to Charles H. Rogers, curator of the Museum of Zoology at Princeton University, for his generous help.

Contents

List of Illustrations

FEATHERS
plain and fancy

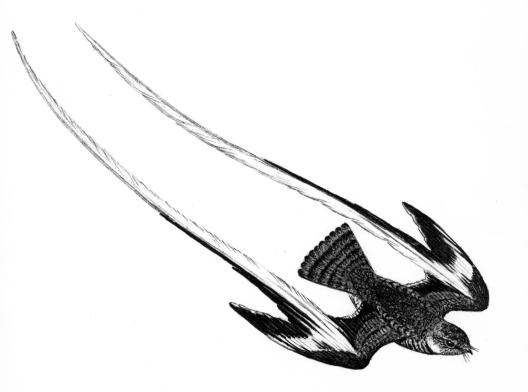

What Is a Feather?

If you have ever used the term "birds' feathers," you might well have been confronted with the question, What other kinds of feathers are there? After thinking it over for a moment you would have had to admit that the word "feather" needs no qualification, as it is applied exclusively to the peculiar and complex skin structures found in birds.

The outer body covering of the different vertebrate groups varies considerably. Many animals, such as fish, snakes, and lizards, have scales, while most mammals are covered by a more or less dense growth of hair, called fur when it is thick, fine, and soft. All these body coverings perform specific important functions. The scales of a fish not only protect its skin but also give the body a smooth surface that creates little friction as the fish glides through the water. A snake can crawl over abrasive surfaces without hurting itself because of its thick, tough scales. In addition, the large scales on the snake's belly help to propel it forward: it "walks" on the scales. Scaly body coverings enable snakes and lizards to live in hot, arid regions, unlike amphibians, which have a soft, unprotected skin through which moisture is easily lost. Frogs and salamanders would quickly become desiccated if they did not live in moist, dank surroundings. This is one of the reasons why most amphibians never move very far away from the water in which their eggs are laid and their larval young develop.

The fur of mammals also protects the skin, but its most important function is that of insulating the body, and especially of preventing heat loss. This is vital to animals whose body temperature, unlike that of reptiles, has to be kept constant, despite wide variations in the outside temperature. Heavy, thick fur, such as that of polar bears, mountain sheep, and Eskimo dogs, keeps these animals snug and warm even in the subzero temperatures of the arctic regions.

The grizzly bear's fur protects its skin and provides excellent heat insulation.

The soft, unprotected skin of tree frogs limits them to habitats with a relatively high degree of humidity.

A body covering of scales enables reptiles such as this sand lizard to live in arid regions.

In addition to these life-sustaining functions, the pigments that form the color patterns of the individual species are located in the scales and hairs. Hence these skin structures serve still another purpose: that of displaying the visual—as distinguished from the anatomical—features of an animal's appearance.

Feathers perform all these functions, but they also have the distinctive one of enabling the bird to fly. Wings without feathers could not lift a bird into the air. If the large flight feathers of the wings are clipped, a bird's ability to fly is impaired until the damaged feathers are replaced by new ones. In this respect, then, feathers are unique, and the more they are studied by scientists, the more fascinating and unusual they appear.

The origin of feathers is a complete mystery. There is no known "primitive" feather—one that shows us an early or intermediate stage of development in the evolution of feathers. Zoologists once believed that the down feathers of young birds represented such a primitive type, but it now appears more likely that down feathers are modifications of the "normal" feather, and thus a late rather than early stage in feather development.

Fossils have enabled us to trace the evolutionary stages of the development of some animals millions of years ago. We have, for example, excellent step-by-step fossil evidence of how the horse of today evolved from a small, fleet-footed mammal, and how, over the ages, the feet of this creature changed as free and movable toes fused into hoofs which permitted the horse to run for long periods of time over rough and uneven ground without hurting its feet. Although we don't know what triggered these adaptations, there is fossil proof that the ancestral horse's toes did indeed change into hoofs, and we know exactly what a "primitive" hoof looked like.

The story is quite different when it comes to the evolution of birds. Fossils have told us nothing about the origin and evolution of feathers, except that quite suddenly—or so it must seem to us, because we cannot fill in the gaps—fully formed feathers, looking quite "modern," appeared on the earliest known ancestor of our present-day birds. This lizard-like bird, named *Archaeopteryx*—"ancient bird"—was a curious creature that lived approximately 130 million years ago, when huge dinosaurs still roamed the swamps, which at that time comprised a large part of the earth's land mass.

Through a fortunate accident some of these lizard birds were buried in the fine sands on the shores of a long-gone ocean which in those days covered much of what is now Europe. Before the bodies of the birds were completely destroyed through decomposition, the sand hardened to stone, preserving not only the skeletons but also the imprints of the birds' fully feathered wings and tails. In 1861 workers cutting slabs of limestone for the lithographic industry in a quarry near Solnhofen in southern Germany came upon one of these fossils. The discovery stirred up great excitement among scientists of all countries, who considered it an excellent demonstration of the main theme of Charles Darwin's then hotly debated theory of evolution (his now-famous book *On the Origin of Species* had been published only a few years earlier). A similar fossil was found about fifteen years later, not far from the site of the first one. Since then, however, no more specimens of this early era have turned up in any part of the world.

The famous Solnhofen impression shows us a peculiar creature—half bird, half reptile, with feathers on the outspread wings and the long tail, and birdlike legs with claws. But its wings also have claws, and the tail is a reptile's bony tail, except for the single row of feathers along each side. Its head, with a toothed, snout-like bill, is purely reptilian. The size and shape of the skull indicate that the brain was also a reptile's rather than a bird's. The animal's flight feathers, however,

look just like those found in modern birds. The fossil outline does not indicate whether or not the rest of the body was covered by plumage. It is entirely possible that *Archaeopteryx* had feathers only on its wings and tail, and bare—or scaly—skin on other parts of its body. On the other hand, it is just as possible that the bird was fully feathered, but that the rest of the plumage, consisting of smaller, softer feathers, disintegrated too rapidly to leave an impression in the sand, and thus could not show up in the fossilized remains.

Spurred by the finds of *Archaeopteryx*, and eager to know more about the evolution of birds, scientists have since searched diligently but unsuccessfully for some fossil clue to the hypothetical bird ancestor they have named *Proavis*, the creature that supposedly came "before the bird." Zoologists yearn to find *Proavis* because they hope that it will give them some indica-

Two different artists' concepts of what Archaeopteryx *may have looked like*

tion of the origin of feathers, as well as of other anatomical changes which started our birds' reptilian ancestors along the road to an airborne existence. As matters stand now, more than a century after the discovery of *Archaeopteryx*, we know only that fully formed feathers appeared on what was essentially an agile, foot-long lizard, and that its feathers enabled this creature to take to the air, thereby giving it a great advantage over its land-bound relatives.

Not that *Archaeopteryx* was a strong or graceful flier. Neither its brain, which was reptilian, nor the structure of its tail or of the breast muscles which move the wings were sufficiently developed. The size of the creature's breastbone, for example, shows clearly that the muscles attached to it could not have been very large, thus ruling out any possibility that the ancient bird might have been capable of strong flight. Instead, it probably glided from tree to tree or from the treetops to the ground, attempting no longer or more strenuous flights. All the same, the mere fact that *Archaeopteryx* was able to escape *into* the air from its enemies and to hunt *from* the air for its food represented a big step forward. Without feathers, the development that permitted birds to become the aerial acrobats which they are today would not have been possible.

Because of the distinctive nature of feathers, the question of their origin is a crucial one. There is evidence to suggest that no type of glider membrane *without* feathers could possibly have turned birds into the superb fliers they eventually became. During the dino-

Pterodactyls, large flying reptiles, became extinct many millions of years ago.

saur age, large flying reptiles called pterodactyls had membranes which extended from the side of the body along the arm to an enormously enlarged fourth "finger." But unlike their contemporary, *Archaeopteryx*, the pterodactyls left no descendants and disappeared from the earth along with other land-bound relatives. Although the pterodactyls vanished many millions of years before man appeared on earth, we do have today reptiles that can "fly." Despite their popular name of "flying dragons," these reptiles are mostly small and not fear-inspiring. One of the best known is a lizard about eight inches long, forest-green and olive-barred, which looks inconspicuous and quite ordinary as it rests quietly among the jungle vegetation of the East Indies. But while gliding in space it resembles a huge, brightly colored butterfly. Hardly visible when the reptile is at rest, its vivid black-spotted orange membranes stretch from front to hind legs, supported by elongated ribs sticking out from both sides of the body. When not in use, the membranes and the supporting ribs are folded up very much in the manner of a closed umbrella. Even though one of its long gliding leaps may carry the reptile forward as much as thirty or forty feet, it does not really fly; the membranes simply support the lizard during this "parachute" jump.

Although they are mammals, "flying" squirrels have structures that function in a similar way. Their glider membranes, while not supported by elongated ribs, enable the animal to make long, sailing leaps. Aside from birds, the only living vertebrate animal capable of true flight is the bat. However, this peculiar mammal's awkward-looking, fluttering movements in the air can hardly compare with the graceful, elegant flight that we admire in birds. Furthermore, the skin that stretches between the bat's legs and tail has many disadvantages as compared with the feathers of a bird. First, it renders the creature all but helpless on the ground. Because it is living tissue that must be supplied with blood, the membrane is a burden to the bat's circulatory system. In contrast, as we soon shall see, feather tissue does not need to be nourished. And,

The flying dragon, a small lizard, uses membranes supported by long ribs as a "parachute."

The bat is the only vertebrate besides birds which is capable of true flight.

whereas torn or otherwise damaged feathers can be replaced, membranes cannot.

The fascinating question of how a species of lizard started to grow feathers and took to the air—with no fossil clues to provide a plausible answer—gave rise to several widely differing theories. In 1915 the American zoologist William Beebe proposed that *Proavis* originally had feathered glider membranes on both its fore and hind legs, and that later, wings had developed from the forelimbs only, while the hind legs, which had ceased to be used for flying, lost their membranes. This concept is no longer considered tenable. Another theory, advanced by a German zoologist a few years later, pictured *Proavis* as an agile lizard running around on strong hind legs, and occasionally taking great leaps, fluttering over short stretches with the help of small, feathered winglike forelegs. This theory, too, was eventually discarded, as there are many examples of animals with strongly developed hind legs for running and jumping whose forelimbs have become more or less atrophied. It did not seem logical to assume that only in the ancestors of birds had comparatively little-used forelegs developed into wings capable of supporting the bird in the air.

Two early concepts of Proavis *which were discarded by zoologists*

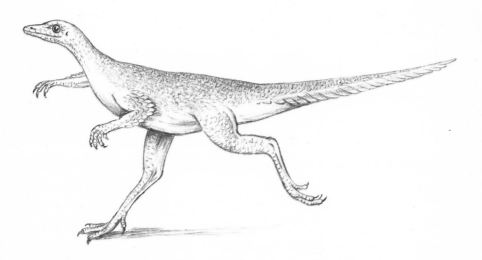

A lizard with feathered glider membranes on forelegs and tail is now considered the most likely concept of Proavis.

Finally, attention was focused on a theory first proposed by the English zoologist G. Pycraft in 1909, and later expanded and amended by the Swiss biologist H. Steiner. *Proavis,* as projected by these two scientists, was a rather small species of arboreal lizard, which had developed on both its forelegs and its tail glider membranes covered with primitive feathers, as an aid in jumping and gliding from branch to branch. Today, this concept of *Proavis* is finding wide acceptance among zoologists.

While we can only speculate on the outward appearance and the way of life of the early ancestors of our birds, certain clues may be found among birds living today which serve as a guide in what may be termed educated guesses. Such guesses are further informed by our knowledge of reptiles—including some ancient forms surviving today—from which all birds evolved.

In Australia and some of the adjacent islands lives a small but interesting group of birds called megapodes— literally "large feet"—which have no close relatives elsewhere in the world. The best-known megapode, popularly called the brush turkey, is about two feet long and does somewhat resemble a turkey, although it is not related to our gobbler.

What has fascinated zoologists most about the brush turkey and other megapodes is the way they care for their eggs. Other birds keep their eggs warm by sitting on them until they are ready to hatch. Spending long days incubating her eggs is not, however, the female brush turkey's idea of motherhood. Instead, she accumulates huge piles of rotting vegetation and buries her eggs in this "nest." The heat generated by the

The brush turkey uses a reptilian method of incubating its eggs.

decaying plant matter takes over the job of incubating
the eggs. When the young finally emerge from the egg,
after an unusually long period of incubation, they are
the most well developed of all young birds, equipped
to care for themselves. Fully feathered, they can fly
almost immediately. Not that megapodes, young or
adult, particularly like to fly. They prefer running
away and hiding to flight, and look rather awkward
and clumsy in the air. What interests us chiefly, though,
is the fact that the parent birds do not incubate the eggs
and do not care for their young, for this runs contrary
to the habits of all other birds. However, while it is a
strange way for a *bird* to raise its young, it is normal
behavior for a reptile. The majority of reptiles also lay
their eggs in locations where the sun or decaying plant
matter generates the heat necessary for incubation of
the eggs. Young reptiles, too, emerge from the eggs
fully developed and ready to care for themselves. Nor
do reptile parents give their newly hatched young any
care or attention. These points of similarity between
the habits of reptiles and those of the megapodes suggest that the latter's methods of raising their young are
a throwback to an ancestral type.

Despite the fact that we do not know anything about
the habits of *Archaeopteryx*, it seems reasonable to con-
jecture that the lizard bird treated its eggs and young
in much the same way as do the megapodes. It is also
probable that the young *Archaeopteryx* emerged from
the egg well developed, fully feathered, and ready to
begin the fight for survival on its own.

Crested head of the South American hoatzin

The behavior of the young lizard bird, too, must have differed from that of the typical newborn bird of today. A possible vague clue to some of these behavioral differences is supplied by the habits of the hoatzin, a strange bird found in South America in the area of the Amazon and Orinoco river basins. The name is derived from a Nahuatl Indian word originally applied to another, still unidentified Mexican bird, and later used by confused European zoologists to denote the South American species. Confusion caused by the hoatzin did not stop with its name. The bird has such unusual anatomical features that ornithologists have classified it, all by itself, in a separate family and suborder. This peculiar creature, a veritable anachronism, has fully feathered, good-sized wings, but uses them only when hard-pressed, and even then flies clumsily, attempting no more than a fluttering glide to the next tree, where it performs an awkward crash landing.

Young hoatzins behave even more strangely. They have two sharp claws on the bend of each wing and climb around in trees and shrubs using all four limbs. When they become aware of danger, they dive into the stream near which their nests are invariably built, and attempt to escape by swimming under water. Leading from the nest is a pathway to the stream—a kind of escape chute—free of vegetation that might impede the headlong dive of the young bird. This is all the more astonishing because adult hoatzins are not water birds and do not swim.

Young hoatzin swimming under water

Young hoatzin using the claws on its wings as an aid in climbing

Close observations of young hoatzins, especially those made during an expedition undertaken in 1960 by J. Lear Grimmer, Director of the National Zoological Garden in Washington, have revealed some additional fascinating facts about these birds. Emerging from the egg almost naked, hoatzins are capable of climbing about in the vegetation with the help of their claw-equipped wings when only a few hours old. Usually, however, they remain quietly in the nest for the first few days. Soon, reddish down begins to appear on the body, and the blue sheaths of flight feathers on wings and tail. The claws on the wings disappear when the feathers are fully grown. However, even adult hoatzins have been observed to use their clawless wings as an aid in climbing around in trees, obviously preferring this mode of moving about to flying.

Not surprisingly, this strange bird has served as a model for artists seeking to recreate *Archaeopteryx*. Artists have a considerable degree of freedom to exercise their imagination in this case, for while we know a lot about the anatomical features of the lizard bird, little is known about the plumage except for the flight feathers, and nothing at all about the pattern and colors the feathers may have had. Thus widely differing concepts of *Archaeopteryx* are all within the confines of zoological possibility.

On the basis of the famous fossil specimens and the clues supplied by both the brush turkey and the hoatzin, as well as by what is known about reptiles and their habits, naturalists have pieced together, through patient "nature detective" work, a kind of composite picture of *Archaeopteryx* and its way of life. In those huge swamps of the Jurassic Age, a bird the size of a pigeon, and possibly resembling the hoatzin, but with a toothed bill, claws on its wings, and a long, feathered tail, lived and flourished, surviving many other creatures of that era. The female probably laid her eggs, as does the brush turkey, in piles of rotting vegetation, or in hot sand, and after a while well-developed young with fully feathered wings emerged. Even so, it is likely that they preferred climbing to flying, and did not hesitate to take to the water if and when the need arose. From such ancestral stock evolved all the thousands of different species of birds we know today, through adaptive changes whose origin is as much a mystery to us as is the origin of feathers.

Years ago zoologists had a seemingly simple answer to the latter question—one which may still be found in many textbooks on biology; feathers, they said, were nothing more than modified reptile scales. While this explanation may sound plausible on the surface, some biologists today maintain that it is most unlikely, in view of the facts revealed by recent scientific research, that these marvelously complex and uniquely efficient flight structures could have evolved from reptile scales. Accordingly, this theory is becoming more or less obsolete. Admitting that we simply do not know how the evolution of feathers began, many scientists now assume that feathers evolved quite independently of scales, and were quite possibly found side by side with scales on the skin of the earliest bird ancestors.

Every aspect of feathers has been closely studied by scientists. While we do not know *how* they evolved, we do know how a single feather grows. With the use of advanced technological tools, such as the electron microscope, many astonishing facts about the feather's composition, growth, structure, colors, and functions have been accumulated. The more we learn about them, the more remarkable these marvels of strength, lightness, and flexibility turn out to be.

Growth and Structure

One of the most wonderfully engineered and complex structures in nature, a single flight feather may consist of a million exquisitely fitted parts. This unique creation is formed in the lower layers of the bird's skin, a process which starts while the tiny embryo develops inside the egg. The full complement of adult feathers begins to develop in the skin of the embryo not long after the egg has been laid. As early as ten days after incubation has begun, the first group of tiny feather buds may be seen on the embryo skin. From the tips of some of these buds the down feathers of the nestling will later develop; the rest of the buds sink back into the skin and remain there waiting for the moment when the young bird sheds its fluffy down. At that point the buds of the adult feathers reappear at the surface of the skin and grow to form the full plumage.

As the embryo develops and its skin area enlarges, a second group of feather buds appears among the initially closely crowded buds of the first group. These new buds will later become the true body down feathers of the adult bird. The last type of feather buds to appear in the embryo are the filoplumes, about which we shall hear more later.

Some young birds are comparatively well developed when they break out of the eggshell. Chicks or goslings, for example, come out of the egg with their eyes open, fully clothed in a plumage of soft down feathers, and ready to stand on their own feet and follow their parents' lead in searching for food and hiding from enemies. Such young, called precocial, are typical especially of ground-breeding birds—grouse, quail, and pheasants—and of waterfowl, such as ducks, geese, and swans.

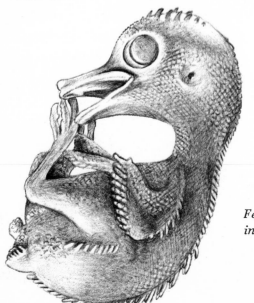

Feather buds show up clearly in this eight-day-old embryo.

Young precocial bird (a grouse) shortly after hatching

The young of many other species, called altricial birds, present an entirely different picture upon emerging from the egg. Naked, unable to see, and completely helpless, these youngsters have to wait in the nest—usually built in a tree or other location above the ground—for a parent bird to come and stuff food into their gaping mouths. Down feathers in this group, which includes all songbirds, birds of prey, and many others, grow only *after* the young break out of the shell.

It takes varying periods of time for young birds of different species to shed their baby down and grow the

Young altricial bird (a mockingbird), shortly after hatching

immature

mature

The juvenile plumage of many birds differs from that of the adult.

full complement of feathers that enables them to join the adults in flight. Although this juvenile plumage has all the necessary flight and contour, or body, feathers, it may differ considerably, both in pattern and color, from that of the mature adults.

Although the plumage of a healthy adult bird covers the entire body except for the legs and parts of the head, the feathers do not grow randomly on the skin, as do the hairs of most mammals. In almost all species, feathers grow along certain tracts, with many bare spaces between. These tracts are arranged in a manner which not only assures complete coverage of the skin but also gives the bird a smooth, streamlined appearance. All the feathers grow with their tips pointing toward the tail, and away from the beak.

The feather tracts show up clearly even in the embryo, where they can be traced along clearly defined lines in distinctive patterns that are inherited, differing among the species but never varying among individuals of a single species. Concentrated along the neck, spine, wings, and parts of the thighs, tracts are found on some parts of the breast and abdomen but are missing from other areas of the body, especially the underside. In fact, the bare spaces, if placed together, would cover almost as large an area as the skin area with tracts. This does not mean, however, that a bird does not have

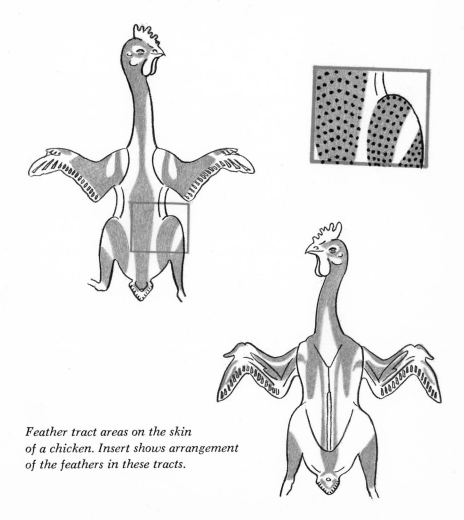

Feather tract areas on the skin of a chicken. Insert shows arrangement of the feathers in these tracts.

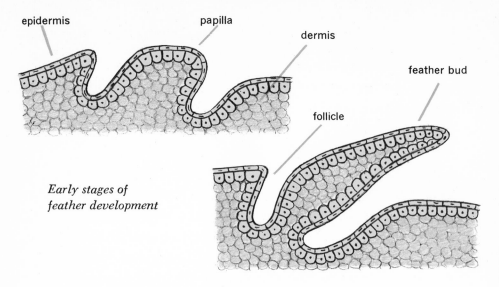

epidermis   papilla   dermis

feather bud

follicle

Early stages of
feather development

a lot of feathers—on the contrary, a chicken, for example, has several thousand of them.

The growth of a single feather is a complicated process. It starts as a dermal papilla, which is a small piece of connective tissue from the dermis, the sensitive layer of skin beneath the epidermis, the outer skin layer. Papillae nourish the roots of structures such as teeth, hairs, scales, and feathers. The papilla thrusts up into

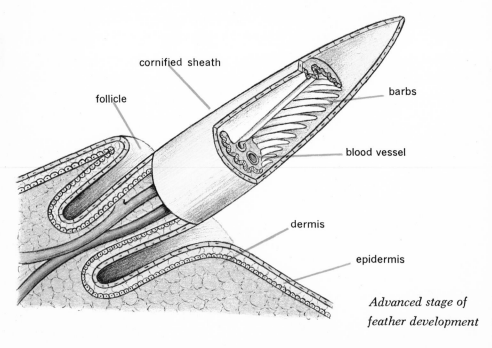

cornified sheath

follicle

barbs

blood vessel

dermis

epidermis

Advanced stage of
feather development

the overlying epidermis. Later, the base of the growth, called the feather bud, sinks into a circular depression resembling a tiny pit. This depression is going to be the follicle, the small cavity which will hold the future feather securely in the skin.

Up to this point, the development of the feather has not been too different from that of a scale—or a hair, for that matter. Now, however, extremely complex changes take place in the feather bud's epidermal cells. The outer ones harden into a smooth cornified sheath. Snugly enclosed within this sheath, the inner cells are transformed into the numerous individual feather parts. All the hundreds of branches are squeezed into a kind of spiral arrangement which is the ultimate in space-saving packaging. It is so beautifully engineered that once the feather is fully formed and spread it is hard to believe that it all could have fitted into the narrow sheath.

The soft dermal pulp in the center of the feather—originally the papilla—contains the blood vessels which nourish the forming structure. When the feather growth has been completed, these blood vessels dry up, and the protective sheath bursts and is quickly removed by the bird, which uses its beak to arrange and spread the new feather to its full size. At that moment, the feather is disconnected from the bird's circulatory system, now being only an epidermal structure consisting exclusively of "dead" tissue, no longer capable of growth or cellular changes. What a tremendous advantage this represents becomes clear when we consider the energy it would take to nourish a plumage made up of several thousand "living" feathers still connected to the circulatory system.

During growth in the follicle, the future color and design of the feather is determined. This also is based upon strict hereditary patterns, which are repeated in all the individuals of a given species, although an occasional "biological error"—a genetic defect—may produce a color variant. The majority of feather colors are created by pigments, chemical coloring substances, which are deposited at an early stage of growth in the follicle. Other colors are produced by special surface structures of the feather tissue. The entire process by which the various colors and patterns in feathers are formed is so complex that we shall leave a detailed description for a later chapter.

The size and structure of the various feathers that make up the typical adult bird's plumage vary considerably. Let us begin by examining a typical flight feather—the type that grows on the wings. The first thing that strikes us is the fact that the flattish feather

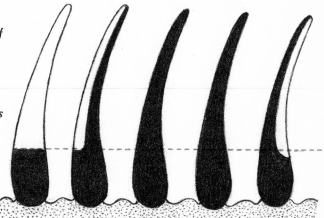

Pigment deposits in growing down feathers of the young grebe that create a black-and-white striped pattern. The solid-black base (below the red line) foreshadows the uniformly dark juvenile plumage which will replace the striped down feathers.

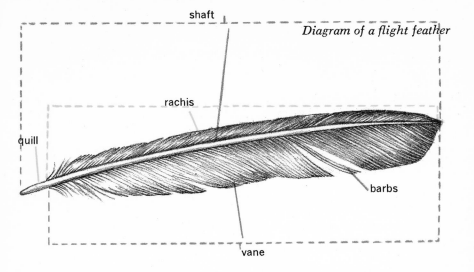

Diagram of a flight feather

shaft

rachis

quill

barbs

vane

surface, called the vane, is divided vertically by the central, tapering shaft. This shaft is an extension of the hollow quill, the thickest, basal part, attached to the follicle. On its upper part, the rachis, the shaft supports the series of narrow, parallel, and closely spaced barbs, the feather branches implanted on each side. Although it is easy to see that there are a lot of them, it is not quite so easy to believe that a single pigeon feather has some six hundred individual barbs!

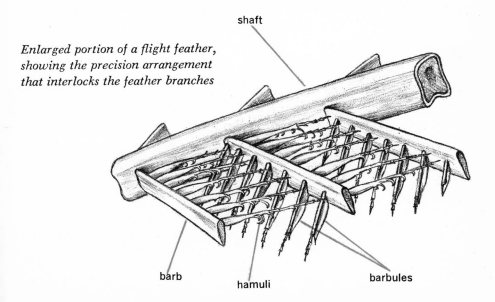

shaft

*Enlarged portion of a flight feather,
showing the precision arrangement
that interlocks the feather branches*

barb

hamuli

barbules

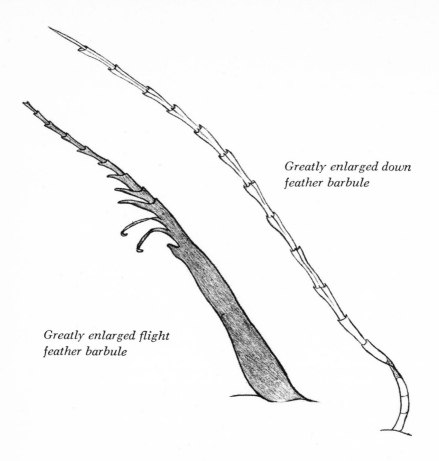

*Greatly enlarged down
feather barbule*

*Greatly enlarged flight
feather barbule*

A look at the barbs under a microscope shows us
that they, in turn, have tiny branches growing from
each side. These barbules—frequently as many as a
hundred on each barb—are also closely spaced and
parallel, and bear at their end the barbicels, many of
which are equipped with tiny hooklets called hamuli.
By hooking on to the barbules of the adjoining barb,
these hooklets serve to join the feather parts together,
uniting them in a firmly meshed web.

While the feather has to be strong in order to with-
stand air pressure during flight, it also has to be flexible.

If the hooklets were fixed to one spot and unable to move, the vane would become too stiff and might easily break. The curved edges with which the barbules are equipped eliminate this problem; the hamuli can slide freely along this edge, adding elasticity to the vane without causing it to lose any of its firmness.

The entire complex arrangement of the close to one million fitted parts of the vane makes a flight feather probably the most superb precision structure found in nature. While only "featherweight," it has both maximum strength and maximum flexibility, so that just a few dozen of these feathers suffice to support heavy birds in the air during long and strenuous flights, withstanding this kind of wear and tear for many months.

The large flight feathers on the outermost portion of the wing have the stiffest, most tightly meshed vane. They also have a thick, strong, and nearly straight shaft. Typically, the two parts of the vane are of unequal width in those feathers, the barbs being much shorter on the outer edge of the vane and longer on the side turned toward the body. The smaller flight feathers of the wing do not have quite so firm a web, but the large tail feathers are also stiff and straight.

The feathers that cover the rest of the body are quite different in appearance as well as in structure. The shaft is thinner and much weaker, and frequently slightly curved, so that it lies parallel to the body surface. The vane is softer to the touch because it is not as tightly interlocked as that of the large flight feathers. Hooklets are missing on many of the barbules, espe-

Contour feather with aftershaft

cially at the base of the feather, which is normally hidden from view by the overlap of the other feathers. This portion therefore has a fluffier, less cohesive appearance because of the looser, more flexible barbs.

Many contour feathers are distinguished by an aftershaft, a smaller secondary feather with its shaft attached to the junction of the principal shaft and quill.

Down feathers have still a different structure. They are usually small and very soft. They have no vane; their greatly reduced, weak shaft supports disproportionately long, flexible barbs and long, thin barbules. Barbicels are missing altogether. The down feather is thus a very light, fluffy, rather formless mass of soft feather branches.

Caring for the great number of feathers that make up its plumage is quite a job for the bird, and one that has to be meticulously carried out whenever the feathers get ruffled or disarranged, causing the web of the vanes to become "unlocked." When that happens, the bird preens itself, carefully straightening out each feather with its beak. Preening is one of the most important chores of the bird's daily routine, for its very life may depend upon the feathers' functoning properly. Smooth muscles and elastic fibers in the skin permit the bird to fluff the feathers at will, raising them away from the skin for cleaning or rearranging, or to increase the insulation by trapping more air between the branches.

Regardless of how well the bird cares for its plumage, the moment arrives once every year when the feathers have to be replaced. At this time, the bird begins to shed the old feathers to make room for new growth. This process, which is almost always orderly and gradual, is called molting, the same term applied to the casting-off of outer layers of skin in reptiles and other animals.

Most bird species go through a complete molt in late summer or early fall. Many have a partial molt in spring, when the winter dress of the male bird is replaced by feathers of a different color. In some species the winter feathers of both sexes are different in color from their summer plumages. Good examples are the male and female loons, whose drab winter garb—gray above, white below—is replaced in spring by a glossy black on the head and neck, a white-and-black collar, and a black back, strikingly dotted and barred with white.

The molts of healthy birds generally take place in a

Common loon in summer and winter dress

way which prevents any part of the body from being left bare. This applies especially to the wings. The large flight feathers of the wings and tail are molted in symmetrical pairs, which insures that flight is not adversely affected. As the bird molts, new feathers grow in each follicle. If the follicle is destroyed, however, no new feather can grow, and the bird becomes permanently crippled. Thus, wings clipped in a way that damages the skin will ground the bird for the rest of its days.

The molting process, repeated each year throughout the bird's life, may require many weeks. Some special plumes, such as the long train feathers of the peacock, take about seven months to grow to their full size. The normal late-summer molts of songbirds such as robins and sparrows are usually completed within a month.

With the molt over, the bird is again clothed in a brand-new feather dress. All damaged or broken feathers have been replaced by new ones. Each part of the plumage is again ready to perform its own individual functions, enabling the bird to adapt to its particular environment, whether tropical jungle, arid desert, or the barren wastes of the arctic regions.

Form and Function

As we have already seen, three main types of feathers are found in the plumage of the average bird. Straight, stiff, tightly meshed flight feathers form the supporting surfaces of the wings and tail. Smaller, softer, often curved contour feathers cover the body and give it its smooth and streamlined look. Small, loose, fluffy down feathers make up the first plumage of young birds, and are also present beneath the contour feathers next to the skin of many adult birds, especially waterfowl such as ducks and geese.

In addition to these three main types, a fourth type, called filoplumes, is usually found sparsely distributed over the body. These minute hairlike feathers grow in clusters around the follicles of some contour feathers. Each filoplume has a long, threadlike shaft without feather branches except at the very tip, from which a few weak barbs and barbules grow. The function of the filoplumes is not known. A fifth, comparatively rare feather type, the bristle, is believed to serve as an organ of touch. Looking a bit like whiskers, bristles are found around the base of the bill in nightjars, flycatchers, and a number of other species.

On the other hand, there is no guesswork involved about the functions served by the three main feather types, which have been studied in detail by biologists.

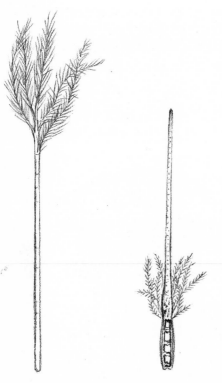

Filoplume and bristle. Not much is known about the functions served by these feather types.

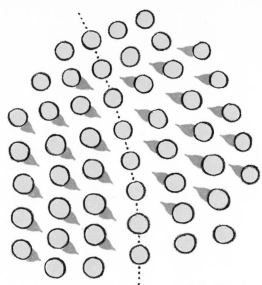

*Filoplumes (shown in red) develop
close to certain contour feather buds
(shown in yellow)*

The feathers of the wings and tail enable the bird to fly. The long flight feathers of the wing are called primaries, because to them falls the main burden of supporting the bird in the air and moving it forward in flight. These, then, are the feathers which, if clipped or pulled out, will temporarily cripple the bird.

*Head of goatsucker
showing its "mustache"
of bristles*

Primaries grow in the digits of the wing, the part that is analogous to the human hand. Secondaries, smaller and less stiff, are found on the ulna, which corresponds roughly to our forearm, while the still smaller tertiary flight feathers grow on the humerus, the upper part of the wing—the part in humans between the elbow and the shoulder.

When the bird flies, tremendous air pressure is generated by the wingbeats. (You can test this yourself by

Typical flight, body contour, and down feathers

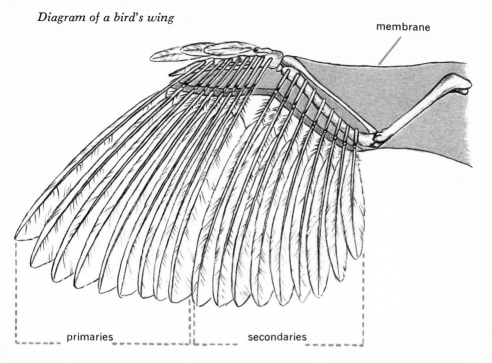

Diagram of a bird's wing

membrane

primaries   secondaries

moving a long, flat piece of cardboard rapidly up and down while holding it in a horizontal position.) On the downward stroke, the air pressure helps to lift the bird up, but if the same resistance were encountered on the upstroke, the bird would find itself unable to rise. Hence, the position of the flight feathers must differ on the two strokes. On the downward stroke, the flight feathers are pressed tightly together, with the narrow, outside part of the vane of each feather lying upon the wider part of the vane of the adjacent feather, so that no air can pass between them. On the upward stroke, however, the feathers are turned somewhat like the slats of a Venetian blind, allowing the air to pass readily between the feathers.

In order to support the weight of the bird during flight, the primaries especially have to be firmly anchored in the skin. Membranes that are extensions of the skin of both the fore and hind border of the "arm" hold the quills of the flight feathers securely in their place. For maximum maneuverability, however, the feathers are so placed that they can turn on their axis.

As a result of this arrangement, birds weighing up to thirty pounds are supported in the air by no more than a few dozen feathers, which at the same time permit the turns, bankings, and countless other maneuvers which we admire when watching some of birddom's most expert fliers in the air.

The flight feathers of the tail, which are also large and stiff, perform a very special function. Birds long ago lost the bony reptile's tail of *Archaeopteryx* with its many vertebrae. In modern birds, these vertebrae have been fused into a single small bone at the rear end of the body, and the tail consists of a group of feathers— usually about ten—attached in a fanlike arrangement. The shape, size, and length of these feathers differ considerably, tails being rounded, forked, tapered, or pointed in the various species. Muscles permit the tail feathers to be spread, folded, depressed, or tilted in order to direct the course of the bird's flight, thus serving as a kind of rudder. Many of the finest and fastest fliers, such as terns, swallows, and frigate birds, have deeply forked tails which enable the bird to manipulate each half of the tail independently of the other half.

It is quite obvious that the structure of the flight

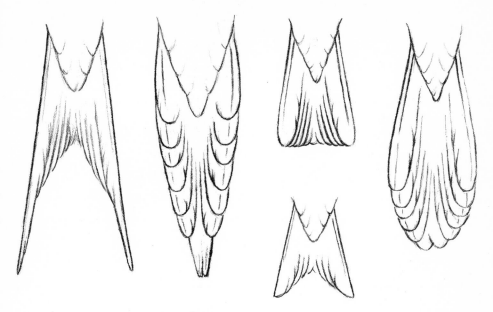

Different tail shapes

feathers, with their strong, stiff shaft and firm web, is especially tailored to their function of forming supporting surfaces of considerable strength. All the same, some special flight aids are necessary for birds of more than average weight. The wings as shaped in a small bird such as a robin or any other songbird would not suffice to lift and propel forward a bird of the size and weight of an eagle or a stork. Every increase in a bird's body weight demands a disproportionately large increase in its wing strength. While a hummingbird, weighing only a fraction of an ounce, needs no more than about 5 per cent of its total body weight for its wings, the wings of a heron weighing five or six pounds take up almost 25 per cent of the total weight. An eagle

Flight pictures of songbird,
duck, and crane

weighing eight pounds has a wingspread of nearly six feet, almost three times its body length. These wings account for a third of its weight. The magnificent flight powers that have made the eagle the legendary king of birds are due not only to the length and strength of the primaries but to the fact that they are arranged in such a way that they can be spread like the fingers of a hand. Compare the flight pictures of such birds as eagles, hawks, cranes, and storks with those of smaller birds, including ducks and shore birds, and you will quickly see the difference. In the large birds, each of the long, tapered primaries acts somewhat like a small wing all by itself.

It is not necessary to be an expert on birds in order to tell the difference between the large flight feathers and the body contour feathers. The latter are not as stiff as the others, owing to their thinner shaft and less tightly meshed web, and they are usually curved, more oval in shape, and often with a vane of more or less equally wide parts.

The loose and downy-looking portion at the base of the body contour feathers is always hidden beneath the overlapping smooth portion of the adjoining feather. In this way, a smooth outer layer which bears the distinctive colors and patterns of the species covers the underlying fluffy and downy layer, which is usually whitish or grayish in color. This layer, by trapping air between the flexible barbs, provides the insulation needed by birds in cold weather. Many birds, especially water birds that live in northern regions, have a special "underwear" formed of fine down feathers that grow beneath the contour feathers. The most famous of these down feathers are those of the eider duck, a black-and-white species found in northern Europe, Asia, and America. During the breeding season, female eiders pluck their soft breast down feathers and line their nests with them, making eider ducklings the most pampered in the world. Eider down is so wonderfully light, fine, and soft that it has been eagerly sought by man as a filling for expensive pillows, comforters, and bedcovers. The lightness and warmth of these down feathers are still unmatched by any other insulating material.

Young ground birds are concealed by the camouflage patterns of their down feathers.

Although the down feathers of adult birds are normally hidden from view, and, like practically all feathers that are not exposed, are more or less colorless, the down feathers of young birds are quite different. The colors and patterns of precocial young are distinctive and vary with the species. Our domestic goslings, chicks, and ducklings are usually uniformly yellow, while the young of many wild fowl and waterfowl have patterns, often in combinations of brown and yellow or black and yellow. Thus the young of the mallard are clothed in mottled brown and yellow down, while those of such ground birds as grouse and snipe show dark brown scrawls on a yellow background. The function of these patterns is to conceal the young—frequently their only defense against predators. For although precocial birds emerge from the egg fully clothed in down feathers, able to run around at once and pick up food, they are extremely vulnerable to attacks by foxes, weasels, and many other animals. When the parent birds make warning sounds, the young respond by running for cover and pressing themselves as flat as possible against the ground or close to objects such as dry leaves and stones. If they remain motionless—which they instinctively do—their cryptic patterns make them almost invisible. Therefore the down plumage of these young birds serves the double function of keeping the birds warm and protecting them against enemies through the camouflage patterns and colors.

As mentioned earlier, biologists have come to the conclusion that down feathers are not a primitive feather type, but rather a later simplification of an ancient model, whose origin we are still trying to unravel. This conclusion is closely connected with the function of feathers as heat insulation, and that, in turn, with the question of how and when birds turned into warm-blooded animals. It is clear that the *type* of original feather—its form and structure—would have been determined by the initial function it had to perform. Were the earliest birds flying reptiles, still with "cold" blood—or did they first turn into warm-blooded creatures which later began to fly? If we assume the latter, feathers developed originally as an insulating body covering designed to prevent loss of body heat. If the former should be correct, feathers developed first as instruments of flight, and were later adapted to fulfill also the function of body insulation. In the first case, the early feathers would have been down feathers; in the second, they could only have been structures with surfaces capable of supporting weight. Today the most noted specialists are strongly inclined to believe that flight came first and the need for insulating the body later, and that down feathers thus are a simplified modification of the early feather form.

To appreciate fully the reason for these conclusions, we must bear in mind that reptiles, from which all birds evolved, are cold-blooded animals—or, to be exact, that their body temperature varies with that of their surroundings. This means that reptiles are sluggish in cold weather, because their body temperature drops along with the air temperature, and all body processes are slowed down. When the air around them warms up, their temperature rises, their circulation accelerates, and they become active. Too much direct heat, on the other hand, has a very bad effect on reptiles. Snakes and other members of the group, if forced to endure hot, blazing sun for prolonged periods without a chance to escape the heat now and then, will die, for they do not have any mechanism, such as sweat glands, through which their bodies can be cooled off.

In contrast to reptiles, birds and mammals have a "thermostat" inside their bodies. The body chemistry of these animals is capable of maintaining a fairly steady temperature regardless of how cold or warm it is outside. Body coverings help maintain these temperatures by preventing heat loss through the skin in cold weather. Thus the hair of mammals and the feathers of birds serve this function. Because of his lack of body hair man covers himself with clothes, often using pelts of animals to keep warm in very cold climates.

Birds are hot-blooded even compared with mammals.

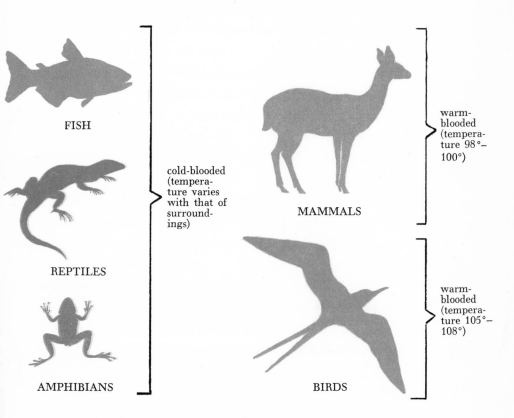

FISH

REPTILES

AMPHIBIANS

cold-blooded (temperature varies with that of surroundings)

MAMMALS

BIRDS

warm-blooded (temperature 98°–100°)

warm-blooded (temperature 105°–108°)

Chart showing differences in blood temperatures among the various vertebrate groups

Their normal body temperature is many degrees higher than that of humans. What is normal for a bird—between 105 and 108 degrees Fahrenheit—would be a fatal fever in a man. Such high temperatures can be maintained only if the insulating body covering is exceptionally effective and the food intake unusually high. Both conditions are fulfilled in the bird. As we have already seen, feathers are the ideal insulation. As for a high food intake, the common saying that a person "eats like a bird," meaning that he or she eats very little, could hardly be more inappropriate. An adult bird eats as much as one fifth of its own body weight every day. To match this, the average person would have to consume between twenty-five and thirty pounds of food per day, which could hardly be considered very little. Actually, birds have to eat constantly in order to stay alive and produce the energy necessary for the movement of the large flight muscles and their generally very active way of life.

The important functions of flight and body insulation are so obvious and so vital that a third function performed by feathers has long been somewhat neglected. This is the function of exhibiting the colors and patterns distinctive of a particular species. Certain feathers in many species have been diverted from their original function and have become strongly modified, both in shape and structure, in order to serve the sole purpose of adding distinctive visual features to the bird's appearance. In these cases, birds have to get along without the original functions performed by certain portions of their plumage. To what extent the feathers of some birds have undergone the extreme modification which alone makes certain patterns and color effects possible is only one aspect of what is probably the most fascinating— and definitely the most colorful—chapter in the evolution of birds.

Colors and Patterns

The wealth, variety, and beauty of the colors and patterns found among the approximately 8700 species of birds are unsurpassed by any other group in the animal kingdom. Birds display almost every imaginable combination of color and design in a wide range of different hues and tones from light to dark. Some birds are colored uniformly from beak to tail in a single shade, but most show different, and often contrasting, colors on various parts of their plumage. Many have no sharply defined feather patterns at all; others are dotted, spotted, striped, streaked, or barred. Colors may range from the purest, snowiest white to the deepest, glossiest

black; from dull, drab grays and browns to the most brilliant, glittering blues, greens, reds, and yellows. Delicate shadings as well as bold color contrasts abound, the latter especially among tropical species, some of which flash every hue of the rainbow in breath-taking jewel tones.

Colors and patterns among birds as a group follow no rules which could be uniformly interpreted as having a direct bearing upon their struggle for survival, despite the fact that the patterns of many species undoubtedly help to conceal these birds from their enemies. As has already been mentioned, the down feather patterns of many precocial young birds serve this purpose. The adult plumages of ground-breeding birds that show mottled grays and browns perform the same function. These earth colors help protect the birds especially during the period vital to the survival of the species—when the eggs are being incubated and parent birds must sit on the nest to keep it warm. This is a very dangerous time for both the adult birds and their eggs, for they are then the proverbial "sitting ducks," exposed to attacks by the predators which hunt on the

Woodcock's "earth colors" provide perfect camouflage as it crouches among leaves.

ground. When birds with mottled patterns—grouse and quail, for example—rest quietly on their nests among dry leaves, sticks, and stones, they are almost completely hidden from view. The woodcock, which also has this type of perfect camouflage coloring, appears to melt into the background as it crouches, motionless, without so much as ruffling a feather, among the dead leaves and twigs on the forest floor. Without a doubt, similar cryptic patterns displayed by many species have greatly aided these birds in their struggle for survival.

Occasionally, the coloring and patterns of birds are adapted to seasonal changes in their environment, as is the case with the ptarmigans, small arctic grouse that live in the far north of Europe and America. The summer plumage of the rock ptarmigan, for example, is a mottled brown and black all over, except for its white wings. In the fall, the dark feathers are exchanged for an all-white plumage, with only the tail and a small area around the eyes showing black. In the snow, these birds in their white garb are as difficult to see as they are during the summer in their brown plumage against the rocky slopes—barren except for a sparse plant growth—of their natural habitat.

Many other birds which live in lush, green vegetation, especially in tropical jungles, are predominantly colored in bright greens, which in that environment are as much of a camouflage as the drab mottled plumages of the northern ground-breeding birds. The same holds true for the sand-colored feathers of birds that live in desert regions.

The ptarmigan changes its brown summer plumage
to an almost pure white feather dress in winter.

In all such cases, the functions performed by cryptic patterns or concealing colors are obvious, and appear eminently logical to us. Much more difficult to interpret in terms of functional necessity are those colors and patterns which make an animal so conspicuous that it will stand out regardless of the surroundings. The huge glittering train feathers of the peacock, the multicolored plumes of the birds of paradise, and the gleaming jewel tones of the hummingbirds, as well as the bright scarlet of the familiar cardinal, or the brilliant orange-and-black feather dress of the oriole, serve only to draw attention to such birds, especially against a background of green foliage. It has been suggested that these bright colors and patterns are an aid to the selection of a mate by the female, but it seems doubtful that this could be the whole answer to the problem.

Interest in animal coloring has received a boost through the relatively recent revival of interest in color in general. Research within the past few decades has revealed some fascinating new insights into the nature of color and related phenomena. Color today is no longer regarded as just something used by artists and fashion designers to make our environment more interesting. The influence of certain colors on physiological functions, such as the depressing—or calming—and cheering effects of blue and red, respectively, has been applied in many ways, including the treatment of mentally disturbed persons. Color is also widely used today in our traffic and highway system to ensure greater safety, and for many other purposes that nobody would have considered even a few years ago.

Color in nature is known to serve a variety of purposes. The bright hues of flowers attract insects; certain insect colors, on the other hand, appear to be "warning" signals telling predators to stay away because the wearer of these colors is either well armed or evil-tasting. Many other color patterns, as we have seen, are designed to conceal and camouflage animals. However, there are also countless instances in the animal kingdom in which colors and patterns serve no known purpose except that of creating distinctive, eye-catching, and frequently beautiful visual effects, some of which have been of special interest to the researcher.

Examination of colors in organic as well as inorganic matter has been greatly facilitated by the electron microscope, with which structures smaller than the wave

length of light can be investigated. Such minute particles are beyond the scope of the optical microscope,
which operates with, and is limited by, the length of
visible light waves. A beam of electrons, on the other
hand, can be used to photograph structures which in
the past have been invisible.

For several hundred years, scientists have known
that colors in animal tissues, and especially in feathers,
are produced either chemically, through pigments, or
physically, through surface structures. In the majority
of cases, color in living organisms is produced by chro-
matophores, pigment cells that are deposited in the
tissues of the plant or animal. These pigments are similar to many of the coloring substances, such as paints
or dyes, which man has used for ages to decorate his
clothes, utensils, and homes.

A pigment absorbs all the component rays of white
light except that of its own color, which it reflects. Thus
a red pigment absorbs the blue-green part of white
light, reflecting only the red wave lengths. Black ab-

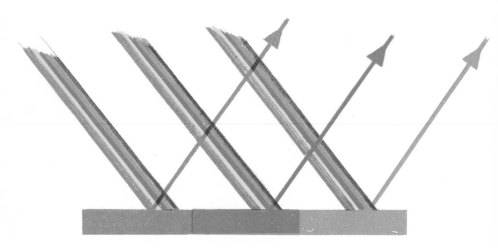

Diagram showing light reflection and absorption by various pigments

Though the color looks very similar in these three red feathers, it is created by three chemically different pigments.

sorbs all the light waves and reflects nothing; hence black is not really a color, but simply an absence of light.

Chemical colors in animals have been the subject of intensive research in the last few decades. It has been found that the pigmentation of feathers is much more complex than that of reptile scales or mammalian hair. A single feather may owe its coloring to pigments belonging to three chemically different groups.

Most chemical feather colors can be traced to one of two large pigment groups, the melanins and the carotins. The former consist of brown and black, the latter of red and yellow coloring substances. Blues and greens, as we shall see later, are produced in a different way.

Pigment deposits in a striped, barred, and spotted feather

Deposits of pigment cells during the feather's growth period follow strict genetic laws, and many of them demand a stop-and-go precision arrangement in order to create the distinct and often symmetrical pattern of dots, spots, streaks, or stripes peculiar to a given species. A solid-colored feather is the result of continuous pigment cell deposits throughout the entire growth period. If, on the other hand, pigment deposits are interrupted horizontally at intervals but are continued vertically without a break, the feather will be striped. Should the breaks occur vertically but not horizontally, a barred or banded feather is the result. And finally, if the deposits are interrupted both horizontally and vertically, the feather will be dotted or spotted. A light-colored feather with dark spots is the result of large breaks and small deposits; a dark-colored feather with light spots has had large deposits and small breaks.

In order to have the same color and pattern after every molt, pigment cells have to be deposited in the developing feather in the same way during each successive growth. Some birds, however, change the color of their plumage in the spring, and seasonal color changes of this kind require that different pigments be deposited in the new feather growth at different times. In many cases, it is only the male that acquires this breeding plumage, which is often distinguished by bright colors such as red and orange. These natural color changes may be very drastic in some cases, altering the bird's appearance to an extent that makes it difficult for any but an expert to recognize it. Take, for example, the well-known and striking scarlet tanager,

Male scarlet tanager in summer and winter plumage.
The female wears the drab feather dress at all times.

which ranges over the eastern and northeastern parts of North America. In its summer plumage, the male is a fiery scarlet-red bird with sharply contrasting black wings and tail. In the fall molt, however, the male sheds these bright colors and turns into a replica of the dull-colored female, olive-green above, yellowish below. All winter long, both sexes look alike. When spring comes, the male changes back into its brilliant red plumage.

Occasionally birds undergo color changes that are abnormal, taking place only when living conditions are altered, as when individuals are taken captive and transferred from their natural environment to man-made homes. This happened in the case of the fading flamingos at the Bronx Zoological Garden in New York. Dr. William Conway, formerly the curator of birds, and now the zoo's director, tells the story of how he solved the problem of color loss that had long frustrated bird curators in many zoos.

The plumage of the more than half a dozen known species of flamingos comes in different hues of pink— from a very pale shade to a deep, rich salmon color. Dr. Conway, eager to acquire specimens of all these species for his flamingo colony, led an expedition to some rather wild regions high up in the Andes, and brought home a number of flamingos of a relatively rare species. With the very first molt, however, some of the newly acquired captives lost their deep-pink plumage, which was replaced by feathers displaying a pale, washed-out shade.

Dr. Conway, aware that a relationship exists between certain feather colors and a bird's diet, experimented with a number of different food additives in an attempt to reverse the color loss. After a number of ingredients were tried without success, carrot oil, obtained from carrot seeds, was added to the food with excellent results. The very next molt of the flamingos produced a plumage to which the full richness of the original pink color had been restored.

Curators and directors of other zoos have since adopted similar diets for their pink and red birds, such as flamingos and scarlet ibises.

Chemical research into feather pigmentation has provided many answers as to how colors are produced by the bird, and why certain foods affect some colors. Although melanin pigments are manufactured by the bird's body itself, red and yellow pigments called carotinoids are found in plants that are eaten by the bird. The bird's body chemistry then converts these plant

Red bird and (below) yellow variant

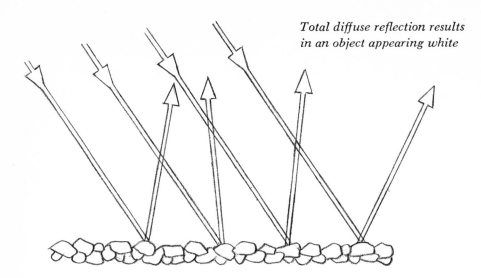

substances into red pigment cells that are deposited in the feather. If the food lacks adequate amounts of carotinoid pigments, the birds lose their red color.

Scientists have found that many birds, even though they ingest only yellow carotins in their food, still are able to display magnificent, bright shades of red in their plumage. Chemical analyses indicate that such birds have the ability to convert yellow carotinoid pigments into brilliant red colors. Yellow variants of birds with normally red feathers support this conclusion, as these yellow variants suffer from a genetic defect which renders them incapable of converting yellow into red pigment.

Tests with red canaries have provided striking proof that food influences the red feather shades. In birds fed on a carotin-free diet the new feather growth was completely white, having lost *all* color.

In contrast, those colors which are not based upon pigments are a product of the feather's surface structures, which reflect light in certain ways. These colors are not affected by food—except in a general way, for a sickly or undernourished bird does not have a healthy plumage—and a chemical analysis cannot be made of such structural colors, because they have no chemical basis.

A great many birds have pure white feathers. Strictly speaking, white, like black, is not a color at all: it is total reflection of white light, just as black is total absorption. As we know, white light is a combination of all the colors of the spectrum, the continuous band of colors starting with red at one end, and ranging over orange, yellow, yellow-green, green, and blue to violet at the other end. All these colors have different wave lengths, with red having a wave length almost twice as long as that of violet.

Ordinarily, we do not see the different colors in white light. But if something happens to bend, or refract, the rays, the light may split up into its component colors, as in a rainbow, or when a beam of white light passes through a prism. The light emerging from the prism shows all the colors of the spectrum. Certain substances or structures, by absorbing some of the white light's component rays and reflecting others, make colors

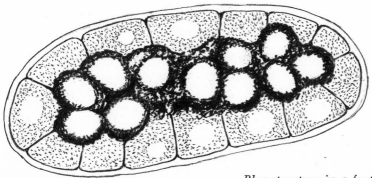

Blue structure in a feather

visible. A white object, on the other hand, reflects all the wave lengths in white light.

White feathers under the microscope clearly show the structure which ensures total reflection of white light. The feather branches look somewhat like cut glass, due to the countless tiny air spaces enclosed within the horny feather matter. This is what biologists call positive white, meaning that it is the normal, inherited feather color of the species. There is also a negative white, which is accidental, caused by one of the genetic defects mentioned earlier. Negative white appears whenever there is a lack of pigment—especially melanin—in the animal's body. This condition is called albinism. Albinos are found in every higher animal group, including humans. They are frequently distinguished by pink or reddish eyes, and their skin coverings—scales, feathers, or hairs—appear white or colorless. Albino peacocks, comparatively rare variants of the ordinary peacock, are valued by many people because the pure white plumage, and especially the long train feathers, lend a fairytale quality to the large, stately birds.

Blue feather hues, with only one or two exceptions, are all of structural origin. From the lightest, palest moonbeam blue to the deepest violet, these colors are produced by an optical phenomenon first described in detail by the nineteenth-century British physicist John Tyndall, who showed that the blue of the sky resulted from the scattering of the short blue wave lengths of the white sunlight by tiny particles of dust and moisture suspended in the atmosphere which are too small to reflect longer wave lengths. Blue color in feathers is based upon the same optical principle. Tiny particles enclosed within the horny tissues of the barbules refract and reflect only the blue wave-length components of white light. An inner core of dark melanin absorbs the rest of the light. If this absorption is complete, the resulting blue will be especially deep and pure.

Blue structure also plays a part in creating green feather colors, for—again with just a few exceptions—all green hues displayed by birds are produced by a combination of yellow pigment and structural blue. Because of this fact, it has been possible to breed both yellow and blue color variants from green ancestral stock. The most familiar example of this is the well-known shell parakeet. Originally, these birds were

The feathers of this bird do not contain green pigment.

green, with a yellow, black-barred back, and yellow feathers around the head. Bred in captivity, a few yellow and blue variants appeared along with some all-white birds, as a result of genetic "errors." Yellow birds had lost their blue structure, blue birds their yellow pigment, and white birds both. Because such defects can be transmitted to the offspring, the variants could be bred, with the result that blue, yellow, and white strains of these parakeets have become well established.

While the Tyndall blue colors of birds, such as those of the blue jay and bluebird, can appear in very bright and brilliant hues, they cannot match the glittering blues that are produced by different types of structures in the surface layers of feather tissues. These gleaming colors, which we know from the plumage of the peacock, the hummingbirds, and many others, are called iridescent, meaning that they exhibit a rainbow-like play of hues. Although iridescent reds and yellows also

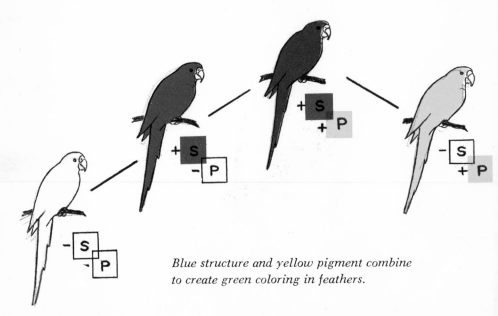

Blue structure and yellow pigment combine to create green coloring in feathers.

*Iridescent feather colors change
when seen from different angles.*

occur, the majority of these colors are found in the
green-blue-violet range. From one angle, a color of this
type may appear a deep violet-blue to the observer. A
slight change in the angle of the incident light or in the
observer's position will turn the blue into green or
bronze. All iridescent colors have a purity unmatched
by pigment colors.

The famed English physicist Sir Isaac Newton, who
first described the physical nature of iridescent colors,
used a peacock "eye" feather as his example. These
feathers, with their multicolored eye spots, are magnificent, especially when seen in the fanlike arrangement with which the peacock courts his chosen mate.

Charles Darwin thought the peacock eye feather to be one of the most beautiful objects in nature. Little wonder that this bird was greatly admired, and even held sacred, in ancient times. In India, tame peafowl are still today found around temples, where they are fed by the priests.

Another bird whose beautiful iridescent plumage made it an object of worship for ancient peoples is the Central American quetzal. Centuries ago it was the sacred bird of the Aztecs, who thought it to be the personification of one of their deities, the "feathered serpent" Quetzalcoatl. Aztec law strictly forbade the killing of the quetzal, and only kings were allowed to wear the long, glittering, emerald-green train plumes during religious ceremonies. In order to obtain these plumes, the Aztecs caught the bird, removed the long upper tail coverts, and then released the quetzal otherwise unharmed.

Guatemala today reflects the traditional attitude of the Aztecs toward the quetzal, which is its national bird, represented on its state seal, its coins, and stamps. Whereas the United States has the dollar and many Latin American countries the peso, Guatemala has the quetzal as a currency unit. The bird is rigorously protected, heavy fines being imposed for killing even a single specimen. Guatemalans are very proud of their national bird, with its bright-red breast, white undersides, and gleaming mantle of soft, golden-green cascading feathers. They consider the quetzal a symbol of the spirit of liberty, as it does poorly in captivity.

The gleaming iridescent green of the quetzal's soft feathers makes it one of the most beautiful birds in the world.

*Iridescent red and orange glitter
on the head and throat of the ruby
and topaz hummingbird.*

Probably the most famous iridescent feather colors are found in hummingbirds. The beautiful little creatures are inhabitants only of the Western Hemisphere. North America has comparatively few native species, of which the ruby-throated hummingbird is the best known. The vast majority are found in Central and South America. Small as they are, some of them display colors of such breath-taking jewel tones that no verbal description—and no picture, either—can really convey their depth, brilliance, and glittering purity. Every hue from violet, blue, turquoise, and emerald-green to gold, bronze, copper, ruby-red, and purple can be found in the plumage of these tiny birds. Many flash different colors on different parts of the body. Thus a combination of a violet crown, shading into purple, and an emerald-green throat that displays golden tones at certain angles, is typical of several species. Combinations of scarlet-red and fiery-gold feather patches also occur quite frequently.

All iridescent colors in animals are produced by a complicated optical process called interference. In this process, certain structures of the tissues reflect light from both the top and bottom surfaces. Hence a light wave passing through such a thin film of tissue is reflected at the lower surface, and then retraces its path through the tissue to the upper surface, where it rejoins the light wave reflected there. However, the wave component that travels through the film, which is denser than air, is slowed up, and will be "out of step" when it reaches the upper surface. Hence the beams are no longer in phase, and waves of certain lengths are neu-

Gleaming blues and greens distinguish this South American hummingbird.

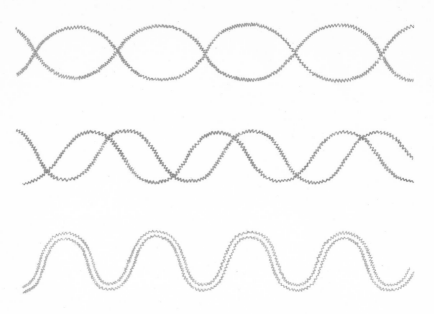

Diagram showing interference of light waves

tralized and eliminated whenever the crest of one meets the trough of another. This leaves only those wave lengths in the same phase, which then reinforce one another. Depending upon the angle of incident light—different angles change the distance the light has to travel through the tissue—and the angle of observation, different wave lengths, or colors, reach the eye of the observer. The phenomenon of iridescence, which gives us some of the most beautiful color effects, is thus based upon a process of eliminating some colors of the spectrum and reinforcing others. This process, in turn, depends entirely upon certain minute precision structures.

Although physical feather colors are not produced by coloring matter, pigments do play an important part in creating them. Particles of black or very dark-brown

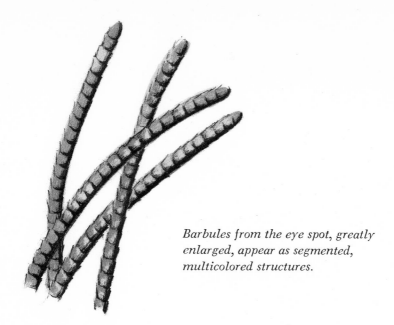

Barbules from the eye spot, greatly enlarged, appear as segmented, multicolored structures.

melanin are the "building blocks" for the color-producing structures, especially of iridescent feathers. In hummingbirds, for example, these complex structures are made up of layers of keratin, the horny feather mass, and tiny, air-filled melanin platelets. This arrangement creates the "thin films," each with a different optical density, through which some of the incoming light must pass both going and coming, with portions being reflected at each layer surface. Without these melanin

Enlarged portion of the peacock train feather's eye spot clearly shows the different color zones of single barbs.

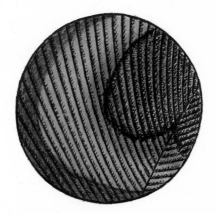

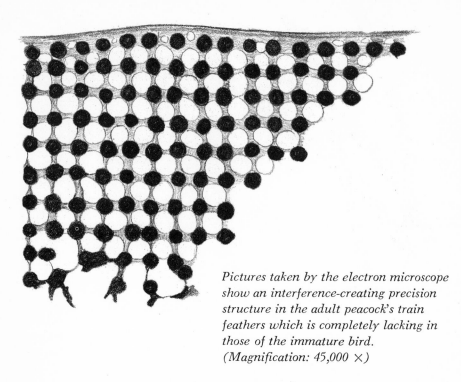

Pictures taken by the electron microscope show an interference-creating precision structure in the adult peacock's train feathers which is completely lacking in those of the immature bird. (Magnification: 45,000 ×)

particles, which appear in other iridescent feathers in a variety of structural arrangements, interference and its glittering rainbow colors could not be achieved. Should a bird suffer lack of pigmentation in its feathers, it will have no iridescent colors. This is what happens in the case of the albinotic peacocks.

The most unusual feature of the peacock feather's "eye" spot is its multicolored design with many different color zones. A single barb may have three or four such zones, which involves precision arrangements of submicroscopic structures that stagger the imagination. For example, about fifteen thousand melanin particles, all arranged in layers that fulfill the exacting requirements of a specific type of color-producing structure, are found in every eighth of an inch of feather barb! The billions of individual particles necessary to create the colors of a single peacock feather must be repeated without the slightest variation year after year during the lifetime of each bird. Changes involving less than one twenty-five thousandth of an inch would eliminate the colors.

Looking at the immature peacock, we get a good idea of what these feathers without the color structure would look like. The electron microscope shows that the dull, brownish juvenile feathers contain pigment particles scattered irregularly throughout the feather tissue rather than arranged in a precision structure as in the adult feathers.

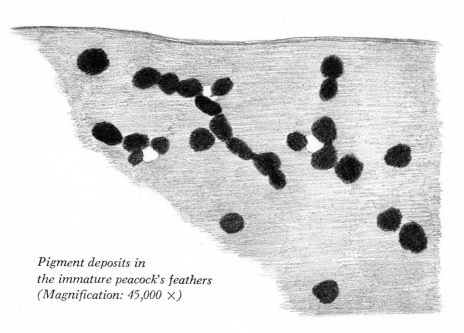

Pigment deposits in
the immature peacock's feathers
(Magnification: 45,000 ✕)

Feather of immature peacock shows only dull browns in an irregular pattern.

In addition to being beautiful, the peacock's train plumes are a perfect example of totally modified feathers which no longer serve their original function of insulating the body. In order to develop their size, shape, and especially coloring, these feathers had to undergo radical changes in structure. The barbs have become long and flexible, and are tightly meshed only in the center part of the eye spot, forming a flat area which, under the microscope, looks like a closely woven mat. The barbules are broadened and turned at an angle of 90 degrees. Because the train feathers—

which are really the upper tail coverts—can no longer fulfill the function of body insulation, a special kind of down feather has taken over the job of insulating that area.

Other structural modifications of certain feathers—some as adaptations to changes in living habits, some as purely ornamental designs—have produced strange feather forms and shapes, a few of which will be discussed in the next chapter.

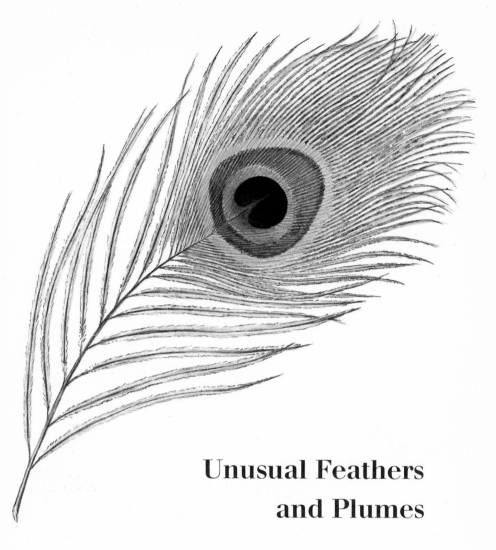

Unusual Feathers
and Plumes

We have seen that certain ornamental feathers have developed their distinctive color patterns only through total modification of the typical feather texture. There could hardly be a more striking example of such modification, and the resulting loss of the feather's normal function, than the eye feathers of the peacock's train.

The elaborate changes in structure and size which produce the beautiful ocellate designs and form the
famous fan when the feathers are erect are so complex
that they represent a powerful argument for the view
that such visual features of appearance are of prime
importance in the evolutionary process. Changes in
shape, size, and texture in many ornamental plumes
have often resulted in producing forms that no longer
even vaguely resemble feathers.

For obvious reasons, modifications of primary flight
feathers involving texture changes are never found,
except in flightless birds. Any change in the special
structure of the flight feathers with their tightly
webbed vanes would make flight impossible. Thus,
while feathers from different parts of the body may
undergo some extreme modifications, the wings remain
basically unchanged in all species that fly.

*The golden pheasant of Central China
has a tail longer than its body.*

Intricate feather patterns of blue-black and white distinguish the handsome silver pheasant of southeastern Asia.

Of the entire plumage, the upper tail coverts seem to be most frequently favored for modification in various species. When greatly elongated, these feathers are properly called the train. Ordinarily, the upper tail coverts cover the base of the actual tail feathers. Although in some species the tail feathers themselves may be very long and unusually shaped, they rarely have radical modification of the vane texture, and where it occurs, the bird has been deprived of its rudder and flight is impaired. Even a long train such as that of the quetzal or the peacock is not exactly a help in flight.

Pheasants, which are closely related to the group of which the peacock is a member, are distinguished by generally bright, often metallic or iridescent color patterns, and long, ornate tails. Such magnificent Chinese and Tibetan species as the golden and silver pheasants

The secondary wing feathers of the
argus pheasant are three feet long.

have tails that make up half the birds' total length. In some, the tail is so huge that it dwarfs the bird itself. The argus pheasant of the Malayan islands, for example, has a tail which measures almost twice its body length; it also has enlarged secondary wing feathers— a rare phenomenon—which grow to a length of about three feet. Although this pheasant does not have the brilliant coloring of its relatives, the delicate designs formed by pencilings of black and light eye spots (the name "argus" stems from the hundred-eyed monster of Greek mythology) on the soft grays and browns of its plumage create a most attractive effect.

Many smaller species of birds display a single pair of greatly elongated tail feathers which have assumed various shapes. Sometimes they resemble streamers, sometimes pennants or small flags on very long poles. The rackettail, a South American species of humming-bird, has normal tail feathers except for the outermost pair, which feature long thin shafts without feather branches except at the very tip, where iridescent blue barbs form the racket-shaped vane that gave the bird its name. Such elegant tail plumes are a luxury the bird can afford without being restricted in flight maneu-vering, provided that the majority of the tail feathers can still perform the function of a rudder.

The tiny rackettail has long ornamental plumes.

Probably the greatest variety of ornamental plumes of every size and shape can be found among a group of birds distinguished by exotic beauty of both feather form and color. These are the famed birds of paradise, a comparatively small family whose largest member is not much bigger than a crow—always discounting the plumes which increase the total length of many species.

Birds of paradise are limited to New Guinea and the adjacent islands. The first Europeans to see a few stuffed skins were the Portuguese who came to these islands in the sixteenth century. Because the birds were so very wonderfully plumed and colored, and because the natives, in preparing the skins, had cut off the legs and neatly closed up the holes, a myth arose that these beautiful creatures were supernatural beings, visitors from heaven—hence their name, birds of paradise. They supposedly had no legs because they did not need them, being constantly on the wing in the celestial regions from whence they came. When the facts became known, the myth died, but the name remained.

It is of course easy to see why these wonderful birds made such a profound impression upon the Europeans. The beauty of their coloring is surpassed only by the variety of the feather forms that display these colors. Shown during the courtship performance by the males only, these plumes can be erected, spread, and arched for maximum eye-catching effect. Plumes in every imaginable shape may grow on the head, neck, breast, flanks, and back.

One of the best-known and most-often illustrated
members of this group is the greater bird of paradise.
Colored in green, yellow, and brown, the male typically
crouches on a branch when it puts on its courtship display. Head held low and wings drooping, it erects the
long filmy yellow flank plumes so that they form foun-
tains of cascading lacy feathers over the bird's back.
These feathers are not only greatly elongated but have
lost the webbed vane of the typical contour feather, so

*The filmy flank plumes of the greater
bird of paradise can be raised to
display their full beauty.*

*The six-wired bird of paradise
has a ballerina's skirt of feathers.*

that their long, thin, flexible shafts support rows of soft, loose barbs that lack barbules.

The species called the superb bird of paradise does not have these filmy plumes; instead, it sports long, velvety black neck feathers which can be erected and spread to form a fan behind its head. At the same time, a "bib" of elongated, glittering iridescent-blue throat feathers is also spread to form a kind of upside-down fan, so that the bird's head is then framed against semi-circles of black and blue plumes.

Feathers from two different parts of the plumage have undergone modification to create the ornamental accessories of the six-wired bird of paradise. It wears an elegant headgear of six long, thin feathers that are almost all shaft with just a tiny vane at the tips, and a kind of ballerina's skirt formed of long breast plumes which can be spread out in a half circle, hiding the bird's feet behind a feather curtain as it sits on a branch. The little King of Saxony's bird of paradise has still another type of fancy headdress: two long, narrow feathers with deeply serrated vanes sweep gracefully down over the bird's back.

Even for this marvelous group, the twelve-wired bird of paradise in display position is an astonishing spectacle. Spreading its six pairs of bright-yellow, filmy

The King of Saxony's bird of paradise, only 7 inches long, has two 18-inch plumes trailing from its head.

flank plumes, which end in sharply bent, wiry tips, the bird at the same time expands a bib of iridescent green and black throat feathers, so that the head is completely hidden except for the wide-open bill exposing a yellow lining.

It would appear that the birds of paradise have exhausted almost all possibilities of feather modification for ornamental purposes. However, many people would hand top prize to a bird found in Australia, the home of so many strange animals. This is the lyrebird, which would be most ordinary-looking were it not for the fancy plumes of its tail. Its fame is entirely due to the huge, strangely shaped tail of the male, which—even though only for a few moments during display—forms the "lyre" that gives the bird its name.

The tail differs from that of the average bird in almost every detail. It has sixteen instead of the usual twelve feathers, and all are radically modified in shape and texture. The frame of the lyre is formed by the outermost pair. These feathers are very long, gracefully curved, and end in black, outward-curled tips. The next six pairs of feathers are brownish above but whitish below; their shafts are straight, and form the strings of the lyre. Having only barbs without barbules to hold the vane together, these feathers are very delicate and lacy in texture. The innermost pair is long and thin; crossing each other near the base, they sweep out to opposite sides of the lyre.

When the male courts the female, it not only erects these distinctive tail plumes but spreads them forward and outward over its head until they almost touch the ground. In this position, the bird's body is all but hidden under a lacy canopy of feathers. This, and not the erect tail forming the perfect "lyre" seen on stamps and other illustrations, is the typical display posture.

That such a tail has completely lost its original function as a rudder in flight is clear. The lyrebird cannot attempt any flights calling for much maneuvering in the air; it is generally quite content to stay on the ground.

Australian lyrebird in typical "lyre" posture, assumed only during a fleeting stage of the courtship display.

Feather crests in seven different species

Normally, the feathers that grow on the head are the smallest of the bird's entire plumage. A good many birds, however, wear crests, crowns, or feather bushes, some of them consisting of greatly enlarged plumes. In birds ranging from the tiniest hummingbird to the large herons and cranes a variety of fancy headgear may be found. One of the most remarkable of these feather ornaments is that of the appropriately named crowned crane, which has a thick bush of very narrow

stiff feathers growing from the top of its head. Other cranes are distinguished by long feathers of the back, which curl down over the ends of the wings and create a tufted appearance. Herons, on the other hand, and especially those members of the group known as egrets, are known less for the elongated head plumes of many species than for the long, lacy, filmy plumes of the back and breast that appear primarily during the breeding season. These plumes, known as aigrettes, were much in demand years ago as adornment for women's hats and other fashions. Indiscriminate slaughter of egrets by plume hunters nearly exterminated the birds before protective legislation was enacted to ensure perpetuation of these species.

A snowy egret in breeding plumage

Among flightless birds, radical modification of the plumage is found in almost all species, but ornamental plumes are rare. Only the largest of all birds, the ostrich of Africa, has beautiful plumes which, like those of the egrets, were eagerly sought after for a variety of uses, resulting in the hunting and slaughter of ostriches until comparatively recently. Although the demand for ostrich plumes has decreased sharply since the time when elegant women wore ostrich plumes on dresses and hats, there still is a market for these feathers. Instead of killing the birds to get the plumes, however,

Male and female African ostriches

a better way has been found. The birds are raised on ostrich farms, and the plumes are removed when they are fully grown. As the bird then grows new ones, each bird yields not one but several harvests of plumes.

Only the male ostrich has the large white plumes which may measure two feet in length and which have been prized by man for centuries; in the female, they are smaller and colored a dull brown. However, old females in which the reproductive functions have ceased frequently acquire a plumage closely resembling that of the male in both shape and color. Thus the handsome black-and-white feather dress of the male with its ornate plumes evidently is the neutral plumage of the species, and the dull, brownish feathers of the female are modifications of the ancestral plumage.

What interests the zoologist when he looks at the huge cascading mass of these incredibly soft, snow-white plumes is the fact that these were once the ostrich's flight feathers. No one knows why some birds lost the ability to fly and with it the tremendous advantage of being able to escape from predators or to migrate from an inclement environment. The majority of birds that have become extinct in the past few hundred years were flightless species, and those that have survived have a very uncertain future unless man takes measures to preserve these species.

Most flightless birds are comparatively large and heavy. This fact is clearly related to their flightlessness, but whether the weight is cause or effect is not known.

Did the birds become too heavy to fly, or did they first lose their ability to fly and then, being no longer limited to a certain weight, begin to increase in size? The upper weight limit for efficient flight apparently is reached at about thirty pounds. No bird much heavier can still produce the muscle power necessary to lift itself into the air. Pelicans are thought to be about the heaviest birds capable of flight. Some biologists believe that certain flightless species at one time suffered an abnormal growth, or hypertrophy, as a result of an overactive pituitary gland, the gland which controls growth. Research indicating that the moa, an extinct giant ostrich-like bird of New Zealand, had a disproportionately large pituitary gland provides evidence for this theory.

Whatever the reasons, the large flightless birds had to compensate for their inability to fly by developing strong legs for walking and running. The ostrich can run as fast as a horse, while using its small, nonfunctional wings to balance itself.

Because the flightless birds' plumage no longer fulfilled the typical bird's foremost function, it could become radically modified. Neither the smooth contour feather outline which helps to reduce air resistance in flight, nor the firmly webbed supporting surfaces of the flight feather were necessary.

Plume of the male ostrich

Both the emu and the cassowary have coarse, drooping, hairlike feathers.

With the exception of the greatly modified flight feathers, the plumage of the ostrich, although soft and loose, still resembles that of other birds. In some of the other large flightless species, however, this resemblance has been all but completely lost. The five-foot-tall emu of Australia, and its bad-tempered cousin, the cassowary, look somewhat like long-haired goats on two legs with a long neck and a bird's head. Wings appear to be absent, for both species have rudimentary wing stubs only a few inches long that cannot be seen unless the feathers are removed. The feathers of these birds grow not in tracts but scattered all over the body. From front to rear, the emu and the cassowary are covered by loose-hanging, narrow, hairlike feathers that form a body covering resembling mammalian fur more than a bird's plumage.

Emu feathers, whose barbules lack all interlocking mechanisms, have long aftershafts.

The odd, flightless kiwi has hairlike, coarse feathers.

The small surviving cousin of the huge extinct moas, which stood up to twelve feet tall, is the strange kiwi of New Zealand, a bird that appears to have been put together by someone who knew little about birds, for it lacks every typical avian feature. Not only is it flightless and covered by the same type of hairlike feathers found in the emu and cassowary, but it also has very poor eyesight—the sense that is most highly developed in other birds. To compensate for this deficiency, the kiwi has an acute sense of smell—the sense which is most poorly developed in all other birds. Searching for the earthworms it prefers as food, the kiwi ventures out at night, looking like a rather untidy dirty-brown feather mop on two sturdy legs with a six-inch bill protruding from one end. To facilitate the finding of its prey by smell only, the nostrils of the kiwi are located at the tip of its bill instead of at the base, as in other birds.

*A distant relative of the kiwi, the huge moa,
extinct for several hundred years, had hairlike
feathers similar to those of its small cousin.*

Despite the fact that the kiwi hardly can be called beautiful, New Zealanders are very proud of their national bird and have instituted strict laws for its protection, for, like all flightless birds, it is threatened by extinction.

Unusual among flightless birds is the penguin, which gave up mastery of the air for mastery of the water about one hundred million years ago. Many other types of birds are magnificent swimmers and divers, but only the penguins have chosen water as their natural element. There are several species of penguins, which differ considerably in size and appearance but have similar living habits. Found exclusively in the Southern Hemisphere, most of the species are restricted to the icy

Greatly modified, the feathers of the penguin form a water-repellent layer.

waters of the antarctic regions. Penguins, whose name is derived from an ancient Celtic phrase meaning "white head" (originally applied to the now extinct great auk), can practically "fly" under water, easily matching the swimming ability of the fish they feed upon. Their wings have been greatly modified to form efficient paddles. Their flight feathers have changed in form and structure, so that they look more like scales. Tightly packed and overlapping, the contour feathers form a very smooth, thick, close-fitting skin covering. Together with heavy layers of fat, this plumage protects the penguin from its frigid environment.

The radical modifications of feathers in flightless birds and their comparative uniformity—especially of the flight-feather texture—in all other species highlight the miracle of a skin covering that developed into the most efficient of all natural instruments of flight. Because of their unique nature and uncertain origin, feathers are one of the most intriguing wonders of evolutionary development.

Diagram of a Bird's Plumage

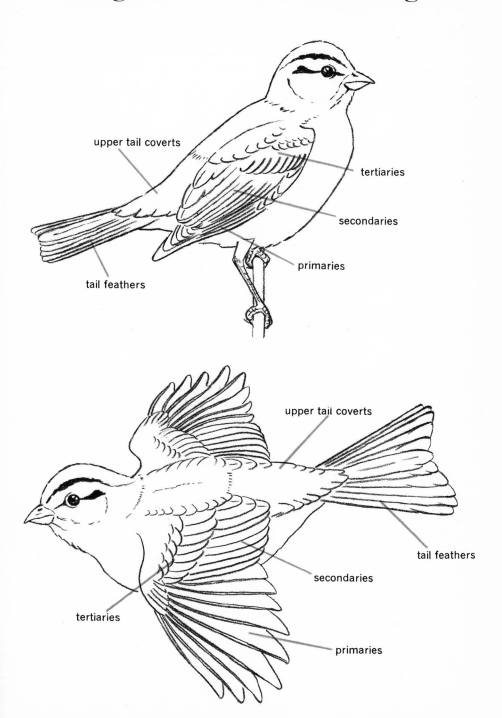

upper tail coverts

tertiaries

secondaries

primaries

tail feathers

upper tail coverts

tail feathers

secondaries

tertiaries

primaries

Index